CONTENTS

Sam wasn't worried about moving house.

MR WALLACE
MOVES HOUSE

Sam wasn't worried about moving house. He wasn't worried at all – not even a little bit. In fact, he was looking forward to it.

But he knew that Mr Wallace was worried.

Mr Wallace had come to live with Sam when Sam was a baby. Since then, he'd slept in Sam's bed every night – which was why his fur was getting rather thin.

Of course, Sam always took Mr Wallace on holiday with him, and when he went to stay the night at Granny's, but apart from that Mr Wallace had lived in the same house all his life. And now he definitely didn't want to move.

He didn't say so, but Sam could tell because as soon as anyone mentioned moving, or the new house, he went all sulky and miserable. And seeing Mr Wallace looking miserable made Sam feel miserable too.

"Do we have to move?" said Sam to his mother, at breakfast one morning.

"Well, we don't *have* to," said Mum. "But we want to. Because it'll be much closer for Dad when he starts his new job."

Sam stirred the milk round in his bowl of Soopa Mega Krrrrunch.

"And anyway," Mum went on, "the new house is nicer than this one."

"Mr Wallace doesn't think so."

"Doesn't he?" said Mum.

"No," said Sam. "He likes this house much better, and he definitely doesn't want to move."

"But Mr Wallace hasn't seen the new house, has he?" said Mum. "And I'm sure he'll like it when he does."

"He won't," muttered Sam, pushing away his cereal without even nearly finishing it.

"You tell Mr Wallace not to worry," said Mum. "Tell him we'll soon get used to our new house."

That night, in bed, Sam did tell Mr Wallace. But it didn't make any difference. Mr Wallace kept Sam awake for ages, tossing and turning.

The day of the move drew nearer. And Mr Wallace grew more and more worried.

Normally, he snoozed on Sam's bed during the day. But now Sam played lots of games with him, to try to cheer him up.

One day, they were playing "Office Men and Ladies" in Sam's room, when Dad came in with a tape measure.

"Just need to measure your curtains," he said.

"Why?" said Sam.

"To see if they'll fit the window in your new room," said Dad. "But I don't think they will. I'm pretty sure you're going to need new ones."

Sam didn't say anything.

"Hmm," said Dad, measuring. "I thought so. These are too small."

"Don't want new curtains," said Sam. "Mr Wallace likes those. The colour reminds him of carrots."

"What about ones with dinosaurs on?" said Dad.

"Mr Wallace is scared of dinosaurs."

"I know," said Dad, "what about a pattern with octopuses and pirates' treasure and things like that? That would really suit your

10

new room. It's got a sloping ceiling like a ship's cabin."

"Mr Wallace gets seasick," said Sam.

"Poor old Mr Wallace," said Dad. And he rumpled Sam's hair. "I'm sure Mr Wallace will like the new room when he sees it. And if he really doesn't want new curtains, maybe we could make do with these."

A few days later, Sam was playing in the garden with his best friend, Joshua, from next door.

They were playing "Fight the Evil Thargons" – so it was lucky that Mr Wallace was having his after-lunch sleep, upstairs on Sam's bed. Mr Wallace would definitely have been worried if the Evil Thargons had been after him.

"Quick!" shouted Joshua. "The Thargon spacecraft is catching up with us!

imum speed!"

Aye aye, sir," said Sam.

"It's no good," bellowed Joshua. "Their spacecraft is too fast for us. Our only chance is to hide in the Black Hole!"

Sam and Joshua dived under the big laurel bush, puffing and panting. This was Sam's den, where he often played "Schools" or "Car Factories" with Mr Wallace.

It was only ever a Black Hole when Joshua came round.

"I think we're safe," whispered Joshua. "As long as we stay in here."

"Mm," said Sam.

"If they try to follow us into the Black Hole," said Joshua, "their spacecraft will disintegrate."

But Sam didn't seem to be listening.

"I think I heard Mr Wallace," he said, starting to crawl out of the Black Hole.

"Come back," hissed Joshua. "The Thargons will get you…"

But Sam was already running towards the kitchen door, into the house and up the stairs.

And he'd been right. Mr Wallace was awake and looking very worried indeed.

"Don't worry, Mr Wallace," said Sam. "We'll make an even better den in our new garden." He picked up Mr Wallace and hugged him. "And Mum says there are lots of children living in our new road, so we'll soon make some new friends to play with."

But Mr Wallace still looked worried.

At last, the day of the move arrived. The house was full of men, shouting and whistling and putting things in boxes.

Mr Wallace was so worried that Sam had to carry him round inside his sweatshirt.

The men worked all morning. So did Mum and Dad. And around lunchtime, Sam watched the very last garden pot being loaded into the van. Then he ran upstairs to say goodbye to his bedroom.

Sam was looking forward to moving, so he wasn't upset when he saw how strange and clean and bare it looked with nothing left in it. Of course he wasn't. But Mr Wallace was.

"Don't worry, Mr Wallace," Sam whispered.

Just then, Dad shouted from downstairs. "Sam! Where are you? It's time we were going!"

Sam noticed that one of his *Krayzee Krokodile* stickers was still stuck to the wall. He wondered if he could get it off.

"Sa-am!" shouted Dad. "Come on now, or we'll leave you behind!"

The sticker would have to stay.

It was quite a long way to the new house.

Mum drove, and Sam sat in the back on his booster seat. It wasn't very comfortable because the car was packed with all kinds of strange things.

Dad's big model ship was digging into Sam's side, and Mum's enormous plant with the stripy leaves was tickling his nose.

Mr Wallace wriggled around on his lap.

Then Dad started to sing. Sam thought it might help to keep Mr Wallace's spirits up, so he joined in.

And it seemed he was right. By the time they had sung about two hundred songs, Mr Wallace was definitely looking a bit less miserable.

"Are we nearly there?" said Sam.

"Not far now," said Mum.

"I'm hungry," said Sam.

"Then it's lucky I brought these special

Moving-House-Emergency-Supplies," said Dad, passing Sam a carrier bag.

Inside, there were two peanut butter and cucumber sandwiches wrapped in silver paper, a packet of salt and vinegar crisps, a little box of orange juice with a straw, a shiny apple, and a carrot for Mr Wallace.

"Mr Wallace says 'Yum, yum!'," said Sam.

After Mr Wallace had finished eating, he fell asleep. Of course, Sam didn't because he was much too excited: he just closed his eyes for a while to make the journey go faster. And it worked, because when he opened them Mum was parking the car outside a house with a blossomy tree in the front garden.

"Are we there?" said Sam, yawning and sounding surprised at the same time.

Mr Wallace looked surprised as well. He'd never seen the new house, and it didn't look

Dad's big model ship was digging into Sam's side.

at all how he had expected.

"This is it," said Mum.

"Home sweet home," said Dad, opening Sam's door.

"Come on, Mr Wallace," said Sam. "Let's explore…"

For the rest of the afternoon, the new house was full of men shouting and whistling and taking things out of boxes.

Sam and Mr Wallace tried not to get in the way.

By the time the men had finished, it was getting dark. There were boxes everywhere.

"Come on, Sam," said Dad. "I'm too tired to even think about cooking. Let's go and get a pizza – there's a place just round the corner."

Sam chose tuna and anchovies and garlic sausage and ham and sweetcorn and mush-rooms and pineapple and olives. And when they got home, Sam and Mum and Dad sat on rolled-up rugs on the sitting room floor and ate the pizza with their hands.

"Mr Wallace loves pizza," said Sam. "But he's too tired to eat any now, so he says I can have his piece."

"Time Mr Wallace went to bed," said Mum.

Next morning, Sam woke early in his new room. There were no curtains up yet, and the sun was shining in on his sloping ceiling.

Sam thought a pattern of octopuses and pirates' treasure might look quite nice, after all. And perhaps Mum and Dad might let him have bunks, too. Then it really would be like a ship's cabin. And, if Joshua came to stay, he could have the top bunk.

Mr Wallace was still asleep, so Sam got out of bed as quietly as he could.

He looked out of the window.

The blossomy tree in the front garden was very pretty. Sam thought it might just be big enough for a tree-house.

And, across the road, in the house opposite, Sam could see a little boy, about his own age, bouncing up and down on the bed, still wearing his pyjamas.

Sam wondered if they'd soon be friends.

"Wake up, Mr Wallace," he said. "We're in our new house, and I really don't think there's anything to worry about. In fact, I think we're going to be very happy here."

MR WALLACE
MAKES A FRIEND

It was ages and ages since Sam and Mr Wallace had moved house. At least two weeks.

The new house was still a bit upside-downish, and there were some men with a cement mixer outside the kitchen door. But most of the boxes were unpacked now, and some of the rooms were starting to look quite nice.

Sam was specially pleased with his bedroom. He'd chosen new dinosaur curtains, after all. But he'd made sure that the dinosaurs were the not-at-all-fierce, plant-eating kind, so that Mr Wallace wouldn't be

21

*Sam definitely liked his new bedroom better
than his old one.*

frightened.

And Mum had bought him an enormous *Krayzee Krokodile* poster to stick on his wall. It looked brilliant.

Of course, Mr Wallace kept nagging Sam about getting bunks. But Sam knew they would have to wait until Mum and Dad weren't quite so busy.

Even without bunks, Sam definitely liked his new bedroom better than his old one. He liked the new garden better, too, because the long grass under the little apple tree was full of frogs.

And, best of all, Sam's new road had a sweetshop on the corner.

In fact, there was only one thing Sam didn't like about his new house. It wasn't next door to Joshua's.

Sam and Joshua had been friends ever since they were babies. They'd played together nearly every day. And they'd invented all kinds of special games that no one else knew how to play.

One morning, Dad found Sam sitting on the sofa by himself, looking a bit miserable.

"What's the matter with you?" said Dad.

"Nothing," said Sam.

"Are you sure?" said Dad.

Sam nodded his head. "I'm all right, but Mr Wallace isn't feeling very well. That's why he's still in bed."

"What's wrong with him?" said Dad.

"He says he's got a tummy-ache," said Sam.

"Don't you believe him?" said Dad.

"No," said Sam, "I think he's really just feeling sad because we can't play with Joshua any more."

Dad thought for a moment. "Come on,"

he said, bending down so Sam could climb on to his back, "I think I know something that might make him feel better."

And he took Sam and the telephone upstairs to Sam's bedroom.

"Why don't you and Mr Wallace have a good long chat with Joshua?" Dad pressed some buttons on the phone. "You could ask Joshua if he'd like to come and stay soon, if you want," he said. Then he went downstairs.

Sam and Joshua talked for ages. Mr Wallace sat on Sam's lap and listened.

First, Sam told Joshua all about the corner sweetshop and the frogs in the long grass and the brilliant tree-house that his Mum and Dad were going to build for him. Then Joshua told Sam a joke about two leopards going for a ride in a helicopter. It was very funny and Sam laughed and laughed – even though Joshua couldn't remember the last bit.

Then Sam asked Joshua about coming to stay. Joshua asked his mum.

"She says I can, but not until after our holiday," he told Sam. "I'll ring you up when we get back."

After their chat with Joshua, Mr Wallace was much more cheerful. He bounced around the garden all afternoon while Sam helped his parents to dig a little pond for the frogs.

But at suppertime, Sam and Mr Wallace were both rather quiet.

It was spaghetti. Sam tried to twirl it round his fork like Joshua, but it just slid off.

"I wish he was coming tomorrow," said Sam. "And so does Mr Wallace."

"Who?" said Mum.

"Joshua," said Sam.

"Well, it won't be long till he's back from his holiday," said Mum.

"But I've got nobody to play with," said Sam.

"Tell you what," said Mum. "Why don't we ask Jamie round for tea tomorrow? He's the little boy across the road, and he's just the same age as you."

Sam had seen Jamie playing in his bedroom, which was opposite Sam's. He was always bouncing on his bed, and he had raggedy fair hair a bit like Joshua's.

"Does he know how to play 'Fight the Evil Thargons'?" said Sam.

"I shouldn't think so," said Mum. "But you could teach him."

"Mmmmm," said Sam.

The next day, it was raining.

By elevenses, Sam had played with his

fort, sorted his sticker collection, drawn a Thargon spacecraft, built a house out of books for Mr Wallace, watched his *Blimey O'Reilly* video twice, and tried to drive his go-kart down the stairs.

"Come on," said Mum, sticking a plaster on his knee, "let's go across the road and see if Jamie can come round."

"Not today," said Sam. "Mr Wallace doesn't want to play today."

"But couldn't I look after Mr Wallace?" said Mum.

"No," said Sam. "He wants me to read him stories. Maybe tomorrow."

But the next day the sun was shining and Mr Wallace wanted to watch Sam play in the paddling pool. And the day after that Mr Wallace had one of his ear-aches.

On Saturday morning, there was a post-card for Sam from Joshua. It said that Joshua was looking forward to coming to stay, and that his Dad had eaten a plate full of snails! Yukkkk!!!

Later, Mum and Dad took Sam to the park.

The park was another of the good things about Sam's new house. It only took a few minutes to walk there, and there was an excellent climbing frame in an enormous sandpit.

Sam rode his bike and Mr Wallace sat in the little basket behind the saddle.

"Here we are," said Dad, pushing open the playground gate.

"Oh look," said Mum. "Isn't that Jamie over there?"

Sam looked. On the swings was the little boy with raggedy fair hair a bit like Joshua's.

"Come on, Sam," said Mum, "let's go and say hello."

"Mr Wallace wants to go home," said Sam.

"But we've only just got here," said Dad.

"I know," said Sam. "But Mr Wallace is sure it's going to rain, and he hasn't got a coat on."

Before Mum and Dad could say another word, Sam turned his bike round and started pedalling away from the playground.

Back home, Dad turned on the television and started to watch boring sport. Mum put on her gardening gloves and went outside. She seemed a bit cross with Sam. And Sam felt a bit cross with Mr Wallace. It didn't rain. In fact, the sky was nearly blue all over, and Sam wished he was playing on the excellent climbing frame.

He went out into the garden. Mum was cutting off bits of a rose bush, with sharp snippy things.

"Sorry, Mum," said Sam.

Mum smiled. "I don't know, Sam. What are we going to do with you?"

"You could let me have a go with those snippy things," said Sam, hopefully.

A few days later, Mum called to Sam when he was getting dressed, "Come and see what's here!"

Sam ran downstairs.

"Look," she said, handing him an envelope. "It's a letter for Mr Wallace."

"Who's it from?" said Sam.

Mum laughed. "I haven't got X-ray eyes. Why don't you open it?"

Sam tore open the envelope. Inside, was a piece of paper with a picture of an elephant and some writing on it.

"Can you read it for me, Mum?"

"Shouldn't you get Mr Wallace first?" Mum said.

So Sam raced back upstairs to fetch him. Then Mum read: "Dear Mr Wallace, can you come to tea with me today? I live just across the road and I hope we can be friends. Love, Gubbins. P.S. Please bring your boy with you!"

"Who's Gubbins?" said Sam.

"I'm not sure," said Mum. "But whoever he is, he wants to be friends with Mr Wallace."

Sam looked hard at the picture and the writing. "I think he might be a toy elephant who belongs to Jamie across the road."

"He might be," said Mum. "But if we want to know for sure, Mr Wallace will just have to go and find out."

"All right," said Sam, "he will."

* * *

At four o'clock, Mum took Mr Wallace across the road for tea with Gubbins. And Sam went too.

He helped Mr Wallace ring the bell. A few moments later, the door was opened by – yes, Sam had been right – an elephant and the little boy with raggedy fair hair.

"Come in, Mr Wallace! Come in, Sam!" said Jamie's mum. "Tea's all ready in the kitchen." She turned to Jamie. "But perhaps you and Gubbins would like to show Sam and Mr Wallace your room first?"

"Come on," said Jamie.

Sam looked at Mum. But he didn't move.

"Go on, Sam," she said.

"I'm sure you'd like to see Jamie's toys," said Jamie's mum.

"I've got a new *Krayzee Krokodile Slimee Swamp*," said Jamie.

"A *Krayzee Krokodile Slimee Swamp*?"

"Come on," said Jamie.

said Sam. And he was racing up the stairs before anyone could say another word.

That night, at bedtime, Mum said to Sam, "So, do you think Mr Wallace and Gubbins are going to be friends?"

"I think so," said Sam.

"And how did you and Jamie get on?"

"Well," said Sam slowly. "He doesn't know how to play 'Fight the Evil Thargons'… "

"And you can't teach him?" asked Mum.

"I expect I could," said Sam, "but I don't want to. That's mine and Joshua's game."

Mum kissed him goodnight.

"But I think I might be able to make up some good *new* games with Jamie," said Sam, snuggling down under his quilt with Mr Wallace.

*Sam and Mr Wallace did some cooking with
mud and worms.*

MR WALLACE
DOES A KIND THING

The day before Joshua came to stay, Mr Wallace got very excited.

In fact, he was so excited that Sam had to spend the whole day trying to think of things to do to keep him busy.

They did some cooking in the garden, with mud and worms. They made some scent out of flower petals and water. They tried to do Sam's giant dinosaur jigsaw. And then they went and helped Mum make a bed for Joshua in Sam's room.

But whatever they did, Mr Wallace soon got bored and wanted to do something else.

"I know you're excited," said Mum, a bit

snappily. "But it isn't very easy to make this bed while you're bouncing on it."

"Sorry, Mum," said Sam, "but it's not my fault. I wanted to play in the garden, but Mr Wallace wouldn't let me."

When Dad got home, Sam and Mr Wallace were charging up and down the stairs.

"He's been like this all day," said Mum. "Like a dog with two tails."

"Mr Wallace doesn't like being called a dog," said Sam.

"I didn't mean Mr Wallace," said Mum.

At bedtime, when Mum came up to say goodnight, Sam said, "Mr Wallace wants to know what time Joshua will be coming."

"I told you," said Mum, "he'll be here before lunch. I don't know exactly when."

"Can we take him to the park and show

him the climbing frame?"

"I don't see why not," said Mum.

"And can we go to Rockington's and have a Stone Age Boulder Burger?"

"We'll see," said Mum.

"And can we…"

"Time to settle down," said Mum, giving Sam a kiss. "The sooner you go to sleep, the sooner Joshua will be here."

Next morning, when Dad came down for breakfast, Sam was already in the front garden, looking out for Joshua's car.

Dad came outside in his dressing gown. "He won't be here for ages. It's a long drive, you know."

"They might have set off early," said Sam.

"Not this early," said Dad. "I'll tell you what – I'll get dressed and then we'll go shopping."

"Mr Wallace says he doesn't want to," said

Sam. "He doesn't like shopping."

"But he likes choosing ice-cream, doesn't he?" said Dad.

"Two different flavours?" said Sam, following him indoors.

When they got back, Sam helped to unload the shopping. Just as they were finishing, a big blue car stopped outside their house and tooted its horn.

"It's Joshua!" yelled Sam. And he dropped the shopping bag he was carrying and charged outside.

"Watch this!" shouted Joshua, starting to climb out of the car through the window.

A few minutes later, Sam and Joshua had disappeared upstairs, and loud banging sounds were coming from Sam's room.

"Josh!" called his father, "I'm off now. Are you going to come down and say goodbye?"

"Not now, Dad!" Joshua shouted back. "We're playing 'Exploding Ghosts'."

"All right then," called his father. "I'll see you tomorrow." And then Joshua was really staying the night.

After "Exploding Ghosts", Sam and Joshua played another of their special games, "Men With Hammers and Screw-drivers". And after that, Sam's Mum and Dad took them to Rockington's, which was Sam's favourite restaurant.

When they had finished lunch, Mum took them to the playground.

They played on the excellent climbing frame, and invented a very good game where Mum had to count how many seconds it took them to get from one end to the other, scrambling through the tunnel and swinging along the bars.

But quite soon, Sam said, "Mr Wallace

wants to go home now."

"Not yet," said Joshua. "Let's see if we can do it in less than twenty seconds."

"Don't want to," said Sam. "Mr Wallace is too tired."

"Oh please can we stay?" said Joshua to Mum.

"We've only just got here, Sam," she said. "And remember, Joshua's never played on this climbing frame before."

"But Mr Wallace needs his After-Lunch-Quiet-Time," said Sam. "If he doesn't have it, he gets very snappy."

"He'll be all right for another ten minutes," said Mum, quite firmly. "Now be a good boy – and be kind to Joshua."

But Sam didn't feel like being kind, so he sat on a bench by himself with Mr Wallace on his lap, until Joshua was ready to go.

* * *

Sam sat on a bench by himself with Mr Wallace.

When they got home, Sam settled down on the sofa with Mr Wallace to watch his new *Hubert and Herbert* video.

Joshua didn't. He bounced round the sitting room, barking. "Let's play 'Ferocious Dogs'," he shouted.

"Shh!" hissed Sam, turning the television up louder. "Mr Wallace is frightened of dogs."

"I know…" said Joshua. "Let's play 'Fight the Evil Thargons'."

"I told you," said Sam, "Mr Wallace needs his Quiet Time."

"Oh please," said Joshua. "Please, please, please!"

"No," said Sam. "Anyway, we can't play 'Fight the Evil Thargons' here. We haven't got a Black Hole."

The Black Hole was a special hiding place in the garden of Sam's old house.

"That doesn't matter," said Joshua. "We can find a new one... Or we could use the shed as our Space Station instead. Come on!"

"Not now," said Sam. "Maybe later. Mr Wallace wants to watch *Hubert and Herbert*."

"Hubert and Herbert are silly," said Joshua, and he charged out into the garden making very loud Space Laser noises.

A bit later, Mum came into the sitting room.

"Where's Joshua?" she said.

"In the garden," said Sam.

"Why aren't you out there with him?" said Mum. "It's not very polite, sitting here watching TV while he plays by himself."

"But, Mum, Mr Wallace doesn't want —"

"Go on, Sam," said Mum, firmly. "You go outside and see what Joshua's up to." And she turned the TV off.

So Sam propped up Mr Wallace between two cushions, and went outside.

At first, he couldn't see Joshua. Then the door of the garden shed flew open, and Joshua leapt out wearing Mum's special gardening hat, and waving a watering can.

"Look, a Thargon!" he shouted, pointing at Sam. And then he opened fire with the watering can. "Peeyooow! Peeeeyooooow! Peeeeeyow!"

"I'm not a Thargon," said Sam.

"The Thargon speaks!" shouted Joshua.

"I'm *not* a Thargon!" Sam shouted back. "You are!"

"No, you're the Thargon!" yelled Joshua. "Peeeyooow! Peeyoow! Peeeeeyoooooow! And now you're dead!"

"I'm not a Thargon, and I'm not dead, and I *hate* you, Joshua," said Sam, and then he ran back indoors.

Mum heard the shouting, and came to see what it was all about. "What's going on, Sam?" she said.

"Nothing," said Sam, quietly. "But Mr Wallace wants to go to Jamie's house. He wants to play with Gubbins. Will you take us across the road?"

"Don't be silly," said Mum. "You can't go and play with Jamie and leave Joshua here on his own. Now I want you to go and make friends with Joshua."

So Sam and Joshua said sorry to each other. They said it rather grumpily. But then Joshua said he'd like to play with Sam's fort, and Sam thought that was a good idea, and after that they played together quite happily until suppertime.

For pudding, they both had two large bowls of Cherry-Cola-and-Banana ice-cream, mixed with Choc 'n' Chewing-gum flavour. And when they had finished, Mum said they could lick their bowls because it was Saturday.

"Whoopeeee!" shouted Joshua. "I like staying the night!"

But then, at bedtime, something terrible happened. Joshua looked in his bag and found his toothbrush, his pyjamas, his dressing gown and slippers ... but no Icky Baha!

He emptied everything out of his bag, but it wasn't there.

Mum and Dad searched all over the house, in case Joshua had taken it out earlier. But it was no good; there was no sign of it.

Sam couldn't understand why Joshua was so upset.

"It's only an old blanket," he said. "Why can't we give Joshua another one?"

"Because it's his special blanket," said

Mum. "Like Mr Wallace is your special toy."

"He's not a toy," muttered Sam.

"I *always* take Icky Baha to bed with me," said Joshua.

"Poor Joshua," said Mum, giving him a hug. "Do you think you can be a brave boy and go to sleep without it just for one night?"

Joshua nodded. But when Mum had gone downstairs, Sam could hear him crying. He wondered what to do.

And that's when Mr Wallace had a very kind idea.

"Joshua," whispered Sam, "Mr Wallace says he thinks it would be nice to sleep in your bed tonight. He wants to find out if it's comfortable. Would that be all right?"

Joshua didn't say anything. But he nodded his head.

"Watch out then," said Sam. "Mr Wallace

always bounces into bed. Here he comes…"

The next day, Sam and his Dad took Joshua half-way home. They met Joshua's Mum and Dad at a pub, where they had lunch in the garden.

Then they said goodbye.

On the way home in the car, Sam was quiet for a long time. Then he said, "Dad, will me and Joshua always be friends?"

"That's up to you," said Dad. "If you both want to, you will."

Sam thought for a moment. "But I won't see him very often, will I?"

"Not very often," said Dad. "He lives a long way away."

"But I'll see him sometimes, won't I?" said Sam.

"Yes," said Dad. "Of course you will."

They were nearly home now. And as they

turned into their new road, they saw Jamie in his front garden.

"Dad," said Sam, "can Mr Wallace go round and play with Gubbins now?"

"I don't see why not," said Dad.

"Mr Wallace and Gubbins have made up a very good new game called 'Driving Instructors'," said Sam. "And I think they might let me and Jamie join in."

"When am I going to get my tree-house?"

Mr Wallace
and the Tree-house

"When am I going to get my tree-house?" said Sam, taking an enormous bite of his Marmite and banana sandwich.

It was a sunny day, and he was having a picnic lunch in the garden with Mum and Mr Wallace.

"I thought you might have forgotten about that," said Mum, who was wearing her painting overalls.

"Well I haven't," said Sam. "You promised."

"Tell you what," said Mum, "why don't you draw a plan?"

"What kind of plan?" said Sam.

53

"A design," said Mum. "You know, a drawing that shows what you think the tree-house should look like. Then, maybe at the weekend Dad and I could start building it."

So that afternoon, while Mum was busy decorating the sitting room, Sam sat down at the kitchen table with a big piece of paper and his felt-tips, and set to work.

He worked hard, because he wanted his tree-house to be the best tree-house in the whole world, ever.

He had nearly finished, when the door-bell rang. It was Jamie from across the road.

Sam took him into the kitchen to see his plan.

Jamie thought it was brilliant, but he had lots of good ideas for making it even better. So they stuck another big piece of paper on to Sam's first piece, to make enough room.

A bit later, Mum came in to make coffee.

"Look at our plan, Mum," said Sam. "Can you build me a tree-house just like this?"

"Hmm," said Mum, leaning over the kitchen table. "I'm not sure about the swimming pool. And what's this bit here?"

"That's one of Jamie's ideas," said Sam.

"It's a ten-pin bowling alley," explained Jamie. "If you knock all the skittle things over with just one ball, it's called a strike."

"It's a wonderful plan," said Mum. "But I don't know if Dad and I are clever enough to build a tree-house exactly like this."

"But you'll try," said Sam. "Won't you, Mum?"

On Saturday it rained all day, and Mum said it was too wet for tree-house building. But when Sam woke up very early on Sunday morning, it was dry.

He ran into his parents' room. "Mum, Dad, it's stopped raining! Will you build my tree-house now?"

Dad groaned. "Do you know what time it is?"

"No?" said Sam.

"I think Dad means it's a bit too early," said Mum. "Why don't you go and see if there are any children's programmes on, and after breakfast we'll think about your tree-house."

"If it doesn't start raining," muttered Dad.

It didn't. So a bit later, Mum and Dad fetched hammers and saws and pieces of wood out of the garden shed. Sam helped to carry things. Then he ran up to his bedroom to get his plan – and he brought Mr Wallace down to watch, too.

Building the tree-house took a long time. Dad hit his thumb with the hammer twice, and Mum nearly fell off the stepladder. But Sam soon started to get quite bored.

"Can I have a go with the saw?" he said.

"No," said Dad. "It's much too sharp."

"Then can I ask Jamie round?" he said.

"You could," said Mum. "But he's away for the weekend. He's gone to his granny's."

So Sam took Mr Wallace indoors to watch a *Hubert and Herbert* video. Just as it ended, Dad came in to see about lunch.

"Is it finished?" said Sam.

Dad laughed. "Not yet. It's a big job building a tree-house. Do you want to come and see how we're getting on?"

"No," said Sam. "I want it to be a surprise."

At lunchtime, Mum and Dad talked about the tree-house. They seemed quite excited about it. And, as soon as they had finished eating, they rushed back into the garden without even putting the dishes in the dish-washer.

Sam went up to his room and played with his garage. Then he tidied out his work drawer, and sharpened all his crayons. Through the window, he could hear Mum and Dad talking, and banging with ham-mers. He wished Jamie could come round.

At last, Dad shouted up the stairs, "Sam! We've finished! Come and see!"

Sam ran down into the garden.

The tree-house wasn't exactly like his plan, but it was excellent all the same. It even had a sort of roof.

"Come on up, Sam!" called Mum from inside. "It's quite easy. You just put your foot there, and then climb up on to this branch here."

"So what do you think?" said Dad.

"It's great," said Sam. But now that he was standing right underneath the tree-house, it looked very high.

"You can use the stepladder if you'd rather," said Dad. "I'll hold it for you."

"Wait a minute," said Sam. "I've just got to go and get Mr Wallace."

He found Mr Wallace on the sofa. And then he went back outside, rather slowly. Mum and Dad were both in the tree-house now.

"Come on, Sam. Climb up," said Dad.

"You and Mr Wallace could have tea up here, if you like," said Mum.

Sam looked up at the tree-house again. "Mr Wallace thinks it may not be safe."

"Tell him not to be silly," said Dad. "Look how strong it is." And he started to jump up and down on the platform.

"Mr Wallace is afraid of heights," said

Sam quietly.

"He can't be," said Dad. "Not after all the work we've done."

But Sam went on, "And now he says he wants me to take him indoors."

Sam took Mr Wallace up to his room. Mum and Dad stayed in the tree-house for a while, talking. He knew they weren't very pleased with him.

Then they climbed down from the tree-house, and started to tidy away all the left-over pieces of wood, and the hammers and saws and things.

Sam watched them, feeling rather miserable.

Later, when they had finished clearing up and gone indoors, Sam crept back into the garden.

Gently he put Mr Wallace down on the

"Mr Wallace is afraid of heights," said Sam.

grass. Then he put his foot in the place that Mum had showed him, and looked up at the tree-house.

It was no good, it looked even higher than before.

Sam turned to go back inside. But just then, a car came up the road. It was Jamie and his family, back from his granny's. Jamie was sitting in the back with Gubbins on his lap. He waved at Sam, and Sam waved back.

As soon as the car stopped, Jamie jumped out. He looked very excited. His mum saw him across the road, and he raced into Sam's garden.

"Your tree-house!" he panted. "It's brilliant!"

"Mmm," said Sam.

"Can I go up?" said Jamie, putting Gubbins on the ground.

"If you want to," said Sam.

Jamie stood underneath the tree-house, and looked up in a getting-ready-to-climb sort of way.

"It's rather high," he said.

"You can use the stepladder if you like," said Sam.

"Mmm," said Jamie.

"Are you scared?" said Sam.

"Not scared," said Jamie. "Not scared exactly, just…"

"Come on, I'll show you," said Sam. And, tucking Mr Wallace inside his T-shirt, he started to climb.

Quite a long time afterwards, Dad came outside.

"Sam!" he called, looking round the garden.

"Up here, Dad," shouted Sam.

"So that's where you are," said Dad,

looking pleased. "I wondered where you'd got to. It's suppertime."

"But we're playing a brilliant game," said Sam.

"Well," said Dad, "I could bring you your supper up there, if you like."

"Can Jamie stay?" said Sam.

"If it's OK with his mum," said Dad. "I'll just run across and ask her."

"And Dad," Sam called after him, "can me and Jamie sleep up here tonight?"

MR WALLACE
AND THE DINOSAURS

That summer, Sam's family didn't go away. Mum said that moving to a new house was just as exciting as going on holiday, and Dad said it was certainly more expensive.

Sam said, "It's not fair, Joshua went to France. And now Jamie's gone to Florida, so I haven't got anybody to play with."

"Poor Sam," said Mum. "Maybe you could go and stay with Granny for a couple of days."

"Don't want to," said Sam, grumpily. "Want to go somewhere exciting."

"Tell you what," said Dad. "I'll take a day off work next week, and we can go anywhere you want."

"Australia?" said Sam.

Dad laughed. "Anywhere we can go in a day, and get home in time for supper."

"But where?" said Sam.

"Well, we could go to the seaside," said Dad. "Or to that brilliant adventure playground with the Death Slide, near Auntie Jo's house. Or we could take a picnic and go and explore the Forest Trail. There's all kinds of things we could do. You think about it, and we'll make a plan at the weekend."

So that day and the next, Sam thought and thought.

The day after that, which was Saturday, Dad said to Sam at breakfast-time, "What about this?" And he started reading from his paper: " 'Do real live dinosaurs still roam the earth? You'll believe it's possible when you visit DinoMania! The life-sized, computerized models are incredibly life-like: they walk, they roar (loudly!), you can even see them breathe. A must for DinoManiacs of all ages!' "

"Are they really real?" said Sam.

"No," said Dad. "I told you, they're models. Would you like to go and see them?"

"Hmm," said Sam, thoughtfully.

"They're at a big museum in London," said Dad. "So we could catch a train, and go on the Underground."

"The problem is," said Sam slowly, "Mr Wallace is frightened of dinosaurs."

"Well, I suppose he could stay at home and help Mum with her decorating," said Dad.

"Hmmm," said Sam again. "I'll have to have a word with him about it."

* * *

Next day, Sam told Dad that he did want to go to DinoMania, and that Mr Wallace wanted to come too, because he liked going on trains.

"But won't he be frightened of the dinosaurs?" said Dad.

"I don't think so," said Sam. "Not if I hold him very tight. But if he is, I know what to do. I'll put him inside my T-shirt, like I did when that very bouncy dog frightened him in the park. He'll feel quite safe in there."

"Good," said Dad. "That's settled then."

So on Tuesday, quite early, Mum drove Sam and Dad to the station. Dad had a bag full of books and games for the train journey, and Sam carried Mr Wallace.

On the train, Sam asked Dad questions about the dinosaurs. Actually, Mr Wallace asked the questions, and Sam told Dad what they were.

"*Tell Mr Wallace not to worry,*" said Dad.

"Mr Wallace says how can they breathe, if they're not really real?"

"Well, they don't really breathe," said Dad. "It justs looks as if they're breathing because they're such clever models."

"And he wants to know if they're all the fierce meat-eating kind of dinosaurs, or if some are the friendly vegetarian sort?"

"I don't know," said Dad. "But tell Mr Wallace not to worry, because they definitely won't hurt him."

Getting off the train, Sam began to feel really excited.

He loved going to London. He loved the way all the people looked so busy and important. He loved the red buses and black taxis. He loved the noise and the hot, dirty smell.

And he specially loved going on the

Underground.

Standing on the escalator, holding Dad's hand, he could hear the tube trains roaring through the tunnels below, and he felt the warm wind rush up to meet him.

"Like dinosaur's breath," said Sam.

"What was that?" said Dad.

"Nothing," said Sam.

When they arrived at the museum, there was a huge sign outside with a picture of a dinosaur and writing that said, "Dino-Mania! Seeing is Believing!"

Sam wasn't sure what sort of dinosaur it was, but it definitely wasn't the friendly vegetarian kind. He hoped Mr Wallace hadn't noticed.

Inside, Dad left his bag in the cloakroom, and then they followed some more signs until they came to the entrance of an enormous cave. There was a ticket place, and a queue of people waiting to go in.

Dad bought tickets, and they joined the queue.

Sam tried to look into the cave, but it was too dark. Just then, there was a huge roar from inside: "WOOAAARRGHHH!"

Sam held Mr Wallace tightly. The roaring got louder. It sounded as if a whole gang of dinosaurs were behaving not at all kindly.

Sam said to Dad, "Mr Wallace wants to know if there are any small, friendly animals in this museum – like rabbits or otters?"

"I think they've got all kinds of animals," said Dad.

"Mr Wallace says can we go and see them?"

"Of course we can," said Dad. "After we've seen the dinosaurs."

"Mr Wallace wants to see them now," said Sam.

"But I've just bought tickets," said Dad. Then he looked at Sam. "All right," he said, putting the tickets in his pocket. "We'll come back and see the dinosaurs later – if Mr Wallace will let us."

So Sam and Dad and Mr Wallace went off to explore the rest of the museum.

It was huge. But they soon found some rabbits and otters – and all kinds of other animals. Sam specially liked a room where you could use a computer to invent an animal of your own, using bits of different creatures. Sam called his an Ele-Kanga-Potamus.

When he'd finished, Sam said, "Mr Wallace wants to go and see the dinosaurs now."

So they went back and stood in the queue, which was longer than before. After a few minutes, the roaring from inside the cave got louder than ever.

Dad squeezed Sam's hand. "Tell Mr Wallace they're only models," he said.

"I have told him," said Sam, sounding rather miserable. "But he says he's very hungry now."

"Well, we'll have something to eat as soon as we've seen the dinosaurs," said Dad.

"He's much too hungry to stand in this queue," said Sam.

Dad sighed and put the tickets back in his pocket. "Come on," he said. "The museum café is downstairs."

In the café, Sam had a Bronto-Burga and TriceraChips, with a Strawberry Stego-Shake.

When he'd finished eating, Dad said, "Is Mr Wallace ready to go and see the dino-saurs now?"

Sam thought for a moment. "Mr Wallace

is frightened of dinosaurs," he said.

Dad looked as if he was about to say something.

"But *I'm* not," Sam went on. Then he raised his finger to his lips, and lowered his voice. "Luckily Mr Wallace is feeling rather tired. And I think if we just sit here quietly for a few minutes, he might go to sleep."

So that's what they did. And, sure enough, by the time Sam had sucked up the last drop of his Stego-Shake, Mr Wallace had nodded off.

Very carefully, Sam lifted his T-shirt and tucked Mr Wallace snugly inside.

"Come on," whispered Sam. "We can go now. But we'd better tiptoe."

So Sam and Dad tiptoed back to the entrance of the cave and into the world of the dinosaurs.

And Sam was right – he wasn't frightened

Sam could feel Mr Wallace against his tummy.

at all. Not even when a Tyrannosaurus roared, and swooped its head down towards him, with its huge teeth showing.

Sam just laughed, and walked back past the Tyrannosaurus, to make it do it again. (He could feel Mr Wallace snoring now, warm against his tummy.)

"Look over there, Dad!" he shouted. "There's a pack of Velociraptors eating a Triceratops!"

"Poor old Triceratops," said Dad.

When they'd seen all the dinosaurs, they went to the museum shop, and Dad gave Sam some money to spend.

There were lots of exciting things in the shop, and it took Sam ages to make up his mind. But in the end, he chose a Tyrannosaurus with moving legs.

"Won't Mr Wallace be frightened of him?" said Dad.

"Of course not," said Sam. "He's smaller than Mr Wallace. That's why I chose him. And he's got quite a kind face, really."

"Hmm," said Dad.

Sam looked inside his T-shirt. "Mr Wallace is still fast asleep. But I'll wake him up when we're on the train, so he can meet his new friend."

Mr Wallace
Goes to School

"It's time we got you ready for school," said Mum, one day.

"Am I going now?" said Sam, surprised.

"Not today," said Mum. "But soon. And you need new shoes and a satchel before you start."

"Can I have *Blimey O'Reilly* trainers, like Jamie?" said Sam.

"If they're not too expensive," said Mum.

"And a *Hubert and Herbert* satchel?"

"If we can find one," said Mum.

"Can we go shopping now?" said Sam.

But Mum said it would have to wait until after lunch.

* * *

On the way into town, Sam sat behind Mum and pushed the back of her seat to make the car go faster. He couldn't wait to get all the things he needed for going to school.

Of course, he was a little bit nervous about it. But he knew he was going to be in the same class as Jamie, so at least he'd have one friend as soon as he started.

And the good thing was, the school was just at the end of the road where Sam and Jamie lived, so they could walk there together sometimes.

"Here we are," said Mum, parking.

They found Sam's *Blimey O'Reilly* trainers in the first shop they looked in. Sam wanted to buy them straight away, but Mum said he had to try them on first.

All the *Hubert and Herbert* satchels were

Sam wanted to buy the trainers straight away.

gone, but Sam found another with a dinosaur on it a bit like the one he'd bought at the museum, so he wasn't too disappointed. And he cheered up even more when Mum bought him a pencil case in the shape of a space shuttle.

"Can I go across the road and show it to Jamie when we get home?" he asked.

"If he's in," said Mum.

Jamie was in. When Sam had shown him his pencil case and his trainers, he asked him to come round and play in the tree-house.

They played a good new game called "Men Taking Photographs of Gorillas in the Jungle". Then Mum brought them each a Peppermint Frizzle – and, between sucks, they talked about going to school.

Jamie had already been to nursery school there, so he knew all about it.

He told Sam about the Head Teacher, whose name was Mrs Gargoyle, and about the little house in the playground where the Juniors weren't allowed, and about the speckly newts that lived in the pond in the school garden.

Sam thought it sounded like a very nice school, but there was one thing he was a little bit worried about.

"Is Gubbins going to go to school with you?" he asked Jamie.

"Of course not," said Jamie.

"Aren't you allowed to take him?" said Sam.

"I could if I wanted," said Jamie. "I used to take him to nursery school sometimes. But I'm not taking him to Big School."

Sam was rather thoughtful then.

"I'm just going to see what Mr Wallace is up to," he said, starting to climb down from the tree-house.

At bedtime, Sam asked his Mum if it was school the next day.

"Not tomorrow," she said. "You start on Monday. Are you looking forward to it?"

"Mmm," said Sam.

"You'll look very smart in your new trainers," said Mum. "And maybe, if I have a word with your teacher, you can sit next to Jamie."

"Yes," said Sam.

"Is anything the matter, Sam?"

"I'm just a bit worried about Mr Wallace," said Sam. "I'm afraid he'll be lonely while I'm at school."

"Well, you could take him with you," said Mum.

"Mm," said Sam.

"I expect you'll have your own drawer," said Mum. "You could put him in there."

"I suppose I could," said Sam. And he closed his eyes.

After that, Sam spent half his time feeling excited about starting school, and half feeling worried about Mr Wallace.

Of course, he didn't want the bother of looking after Mr Wallace when he was busy with his school work. And what if his drawer wasn't big enough? Mr Wallace hated having his ears squashed.

But Mr Wallace hated being left by himself, too. And Sam knew he'd be miserable staying at home all on his own.

Sam didn't know what to do.

The day before he was going to start school, Sam decided he definitely wouldn't take Mr Wallace with him.

But the next morning, as soon as he woke

up, he knew that Mr Wallace had one of his wobbly tummies, and couldn't possibly be left by himself.

For some reason, Sam didn't feel like any breakfast. So, as soon as he was dressed, he made Mr Wallace a comfortable bed in his new satchel.

As long as Sam left the zip a little bit open, Mr Wallace could stay cosily in there all day – and Sam wouldn't need to worry about him getting his ears squashed in a nasty dark drawer.

Sam felt much better then, and so did Mr Wallace.

"Nearly time to go," said Mum, giving Sam a Chokablok for his break.

"Can I take a carrot too?" said Sam.

"All right," said Mum. "But hurry. We don't want to be late on your very first day."

* * *

Sam was very excited when they got to school.

He saw Jamie and his mum in the playground, and they all went in together.

Sam found his peg and hung up his satchel. He remembered to undo the zip, so that Mr Wallace would have plenty of fresh air.

"Come on, Sam," said Jamie.

Sam put his hand into his satchel and gave Mr Wallace a little squeeze.

"Coming," he said. And he followed Jamie into the classroom.

Very soon, it was time to go home.

At least, it seemed soon to Sam. And the funny thing was, when the bell rang for the end of school, he found that he hadn't thought about Mr Wallace all day.

He supposed it was because he'd been too

busy painting a picture of Mum and Dad, and getting to know Miss Williams, and making a spaceship out of KonStrux, and looking for speckly newts in the school pond, and playing with Jamie in the playground, and making friends with Nathan and Ella and Briony, and listening to a story about a cheetah and a hippopotamus, and making glue out of flour and water … and doing all kinds of other interesting school things.

He felt a bit worried when he remembered Mr Wallace. So he hurried to his peg to look in his satchel. But it was all right, Mr Wallace was fast asleep. And it looked to Sam as if he'd eaten some of his carrot.

"Can you come to my house for tea?" said Jamie. "I've got a new *Hubert and Herbert* video."

"I'll ask my Mum," said Sam, picking up

Mr Wallace was fast asleep.

his satchel and running out into the playground, where she was waiting for him.

Next day, Mum said she'd take Sam across to Jamie's house, so they could walk to school together.

Just as they were going out of the front door, Sam remembered something. He ran upstairs, and came back down a few seconds later with Mr Wallace.

"Is Mr Wallace going with you?" said Mum.

"Oh no," said Sam. "Jamie had a good idea. He said Mr Wallace could go and keep Gubbins company at his house. They're friends, you know."

"Yes," said Mum. "I know."

"Come on, Mr Wallace," said Sam. "I can't wait to get to school."

THE

END

THE BEST DAY OF THE WEEK
Hannah Cole

For Angela and her older sister Carole, the best day of the week is Saturday. That's the day they (and Angela's bear Fergus) go to visit Granny and Grandpa in their house by the river. These warm-hearted stories tell of three very different but unforgettable Saturdays: a happy, rainy day of hopscotch, a sad day at the hospital and a magical day at the theatre with a pantomime witch.

ZENOBIA AND MOUSE
Vivian French

In many ways Zenobia is a quite ordinary little girl. She goes to school, she likes making a mess, she doesn't much like baths and, of course, she has a best friend. But Zenobia's best friend is very special. His name is Mouse and he has a tail, a furry body, tattered pink ears, button eyes that shine and wink – and, most extraordinary of all, he talks! Read all about Zenobia and Mouse in these six amusing and acutely observed stories.

IN CRACK WILLOW WOOD
Sam McBratney

Harvey Stoat and his friends Olivia Vole, Charity Rabbit, Badger and Hog all go to the same school in Crack Willow Wood. So too does Billy Weasel, who is always making a nuisance of himself. Read how he nearly gets Charity into trouble over an important parcel and turns up uninvited at Harvey's birthday party; how Badger gets a bad case of the Tuesday blues and how Harvey tries to make time stand still, discovers an old skull and learns some home truths about the tooth fairies!

These five enchanting woodland stories, by the author of the acclaimed *Guess How Much I Love You*, are ideal for reading aloud.

MORE WALKER STORYBOOKS

For You to Enjoy

☐ 0-7445-5467-5   *The Best Day of the Week*
Hannah Cole/John Prater   £3.50

☐ 0-7445-5400-4   *The Owl Tree*
Jenny Nimmo/Anthony Lewis
£3.50

☐ 0-7445-5401-2   *The Silver Egg*
Vivien Alcock/Ivan Bates   £3.50

☐ 0-7445-5482-9   *In Crack Willow Wood*
Sam McBratney/Ivan Bates
£3.50

☐ 0-7445-5481-0   *Clever Cakes*
Michael Rosen/Caroline Holden
£3.50

☐ 0-7445-5451-9   *Zenobia and Mouse*
Vivian French/Duncan Smith
£3.50

☐ 0-7445-5275-3   *Hazel the Guinea-pig*
A.N. Wilson/Jonathan Heale
£3.50

**Walker Paperbacks are available from most booksellers,
or by post from B.B.C.S., P.O. Box 941, Hull, North Humberside HU1 3YQ**

24 hour telephone credit card line 01482 224626

To order, send: Title, author, ISBN number and price for each book ordered, your full
name and address, cheque or postal order payable to BBCS for the total amount and allow
the following for postage and packing: UK and BFPO: £1.00 for the first book, and 50p
for each additional book to a maximum of £3.50. Overseas and Eire: £2.00 for the first
book, £1.00 for the second and 50p for each additional book.

Prices and availability are subject to change without notice.

Name _____

Address _____

_____